little Miss Somersault

by Roger H

PSS!
PRICE STERN SLOAN
An Imprint of Penguin Group (USA) Inc.

Little Miss Somersault is the sort of person who doesn't just go out for a walk.

Oh no, not Little Miss Somersault.

She is too full of energy for that.

Rather than walking everywhere,
she cartwheels everywhere!

Little Miss Somersault doesn't just sit in a chair.

She balances on the back of it.

Little Miss Somersault doesn't walk around things.

She jumps right over them!

And instead of answering the telephone like you
or I might, she . . .

well, just look at her!

The other day, when she was cartwheeling past Mr. Worry's house, he called out to her. "There's a leaf on my roof. Could you please get it for me?" he asked.

Mr. Worry had spent the whole morning worrying that the leaf might make his roof fall in!

"I have a long ladder," he added.

Little Miss Somersault said, "I don't need a ladder." And, quick as a flash, she climbed on top of Mr. Worry's house and got the leaf off.

A little further down the road, Little Miss Somersault came to Mr. Skinny's house.

Mr. Skinny was at the top of a ladder painting his roof.

Unfortunately, Mr. Bump came around the corner and walked under the ladder.

Or rather, he tried to walk under the ladder, but being Mr. Bump, he walked straight into it.

BUMP!

And you can see what happened!

Little Miss Somersault saw it all happen.

And without even thinking about the fallen ladder, she climbed to the top of Mr. Skinny's house, tucked him under her arm, and carried him safely to the ground.

He wasn't very heavy!

By the next morning, everybody had heard about Little Miss Somersault's daring deeds.

The phone rang. It was Mr. Uppity. "There's an umbrella stuck in my chimney. I hear you're good at climbing roofs. I'll expect you here in five minutes!"

Mr. Uppity's house is one of the biggest houses you will ever see.

"To climb to the top of Mr. Uppity's house will be a real challenge," said Little Miss Somersault.

It took no time at all for Little Miss Somersault to climb onto Mr. Uppity's roof.

"That was easy," she said as she balanced on the chimney.

Then she looked down at the ground, far below her.

That was the last thing she should have done. Little Miss Somersault suddenly felt dizzy. Her knees began to tremble. Everything began to spin 'round and 'round.

Little Miss Somersault discovered she was afraid of heights!

Luckily, Mr. Tickle happened to be passing by.

He stretched out one of his extraordinarily long arms.

Did he want to tickle Little Miss Somersault?

Of course he did!

But not before he had brought her safely back down to the ground.

"Stop it!" laughed Little Miss Somersault.
"I promise I won't do anything so foolish again!"

And off went Mr. Tickle to look for somebody else to tickle.

That evening, Little Miss Somersault was
sitting—that's right, sitting—in her armchair.

Suddenly the telephone rang.

"My hat has blown off," said a voice at the other end.
"And it's landed on the roof of my house.
Could you—"

Little Miss Somersault's face turned pale.

"Who is this?" she asked in a trembling voice.

"It's Mr. Small," said Mr. Small.

Little Miss Somersault breathed a huge sigh of relief.

"I'll be there in five minutes!" she said.

And off she somersaulted!

ISBN 978-0-8431-7815-9   22 21 20 19 18 17 16 15 14

MR. MEN   **LITTLE MISS**

PSS!
PRICE STERN SLOAN

ALWAYS LEARNING   PEARSON

Little Miss
Bossy

Little Miss
Naughty

Little Miss
Neat

Little Miss
Sunshine

Little Miss
Tiny

Little Miss
Trouble

Little Miss
Giggles

Little Miss
Helpful

Little Miss
Magic

Little Miss
Shy

Little Miss
Splendid

Little Miss
Twins

Little Miss
Chatterbox

Little Miss
Ditzy

Little Miss
Late

Little Miss
Lucky

Little Miss
Scatterbrain

Little Miss
Star

Little Miss
Busy

Little Miss
Quick

Little Miss
Wise

Little Miss
Tidy

Little Miss
Greedy

Little Miss
Fickle

Little Miss
Brainy

Little Miss
Stubborn

Little Miss
Curious

Little Miss

Little Miss

$3.99 US
($4.99 CAN)

PSS!
PRICE STERN SLOAN

penguin.com/youngreaders

Little Miss
Somersault

Little Miss
Scary

Little Miss
Bad

Little Miss
Whoops

EAN

9 780843 178159

50399